# Piglet Meets a Heffalump

LIBRARIES NI
WITHDRAWN FROM STOCK

EGMONT

# EGMONT

*We bring stories to life*

*Piglet Meets a Heffalump* adapted from
*Winnie-the-Pooh*, first published 1926
Published in this edition in 2016 by Egmont UK Limited
The Yellow Building, 1 Nicholas Road, London W11 4AN
www.egmont.co.uk

Text by A.A.Milne copyright © Trustees of the Pooh Properties
Line illustrations copyright © E.H.Shepard
Colouring of the illustrations copyright © 1970 and 1973
E.H.Shepard and Egmont UK Limited

ISBN 978 1 4052 8134 8
34783/5

Printed in Malaysia

All rights reserved. No part of this publication may be reproduced,
stored in a retrieval system, or transmitted, in any means, electronic,
mechanical, photocopying, recording or otherwise, without the prior
permission of the publisher and copyright owner.

Stay safe online. Egmont is not responsible for content hosted by third parties.

# Piglet
# Meets a
# Heffalump

## A.A.MILNE
*with decorations by* E.H.Shepard

ORIGINAL AND UNABRIDGED

One day, when Christopher Robin and Winnie-the-Pooh and Piglet were all talking together, Christopher Robin finished the mouthful he was eating and said carelessly: 'I saw a Heffalump to-day, Piglet.'

'What was it doing?' asked Piglet.

'Just lumping along,' said Christopher Robin. 'I don't think it saw *me*.'

'I saw one once,' said Piglet. 'At least, I think I did,' he said. 'Only perhaps it wasn't.'

'So did I,' said Pooh, wondering what a Heffalump was like.

'You don't often see them,' said Christopher Robin carelessly.

'Not now,' said Piglet.

'Not at this time of year,' said Pooh.

Then they all talked about something else, until it was time for Pooh and Piglet to go home together. At first as they stumped along the path which edged the Hundred Acre Wood, they didn't say much to each other; but when they came to the stream, and had helped each other across the stepping stones, and were able to walk side by side again over the heather, they began to talk in a friendly way about this and that, and Piglet said, 'If you see what I mean, Pooh,' and Pooh said, 'It's just what I think myself, Piglet,' and Piglet said, 'But, on the other hand, Pooh, we must remember,' and Pooh said, 'Quite true, Piglet, although I had forgotten it for the moment.' And then, just as they came to the Six Pine Trees,

Pooh looked round to see that nobody else was listening, and said in a very solemn voice:

'Piglet, I have decided something.'

'What have you decided, Pooh?'

'I have decided to catch a Heffalump.'

Pooh nodded his head several times as he said this, and waited for Piglet to say 'How?' or 'Pooh, you couldn't!' or something helpful of that sort, but Piglet said nothing. The fact was Piglet was wishing that he had thought about it first.

'I shall do it,' said Pooh, after waiting a little longer, 'by means of a trap. And it must be a Cunning Trap, so you will have to help me, Piglet.'

'Pooh,' said Piglet, feeling quite happy again now, 'I will.' And then he said, 'How shall we do it?' and Pooh said, 'That's just it. How?' And then they sat down together to think it out.

Pooh's first idea was that they should dig a Very Deep Pit, and then the

Heffalump would come along and fall into the Pit, and –

'Why?' said Piglet.

'Why what?' said Pooh.

'Why would he fall in?'

Pooh rubbed his nose with his paw, and said that the Heffalump might be walking along, humming a little song, and looking up at the sky, wondering if it would rain, and so he wouldn't see the Very Deep Pit until he was halfway down, when it would be too late.

Piglet said that this was a very good Trap, but supposing it were raining already?

Pooh rubbed his nose again, and said that he hadn't thought of that. And then he brightened up, and said that, if it were raining already, the Heffalump would be looking at the sky wondering if it would clear up, and so he wouldn't see the Very Deep Pit until he was halfway down ... When it would be too late.

Piglet said that, now that this

point had been explained, he thought it was a Cunning Trap.

Pooh was very proud when he heard this, and he felt that the Heffalump was as good as caught already, but there was just one other thing which had to be thought about, and it was this. *Where should they dig the Very Deep Pit?*

Piglet said that the best place would be somewhere where a Heffalump was, just before he fell into it, only about a foot further on.

'But then he would see us digging it,' said Pooh.

'Not if he was looking at the sky.'

'He would Suspect,' said Pooh, 'if he happened to look down.' He thought for a long time and then added sadly, 'It isn't as easy as I thought. I suppose that's why Heffalumps hardly ever get caught.'

'That must be it,' said Piglet.

They sighed and got up; and when they had taken a few gorse prickles out of themselves they sat down again; and all the time Pooh was saying to himself, 'If only I could *think* of something!' For he felt sure that a Very Clever Brain could catch a Heffalump if only he knew the right way to go about it.

'Suppose,' he said to Piglet, '*you* wanted to catch *me*, how would you do it?'

'Well,' said Piglet, 'I should do it like this. I should make a Trap, and I should put a Jar of Honey in the Trap, and you would smell it, and you would go in after it, and –'

'And I would go in after it,' said Pooh excitedly, 'only very carefully so as not to hurt myself, and I would get to the Jar of Honey, and I should lick round the edges first of all, pretending that there wasn't any more, you know, and then I should walk away and think about it a little, and then I should come back and start licking in the middle of the jar, and then –'

'Yes, well never mind about that. There you would be, and there I should catch you. Now the first thing to think of is, What do Heffalumps like? I should think acorns, shouldn't you? We'll get a lot of – I say, wake up, Pooh!'

Pooh, who had gone into a happy dream, woke up with a start, and said that Honey was a much more trappy thing than Haycorns. Piglet didn't think so; and they were just going to argue about it, when Piglet remembered that, if they put acorns in the Trap, *he* would have to find the acorns, but if they put honey, then Pooh would have to give up some of his own honey, so he said, 'All right, honey then,' just as Pooh remembered it too, and was going to say, 'All right, haycorns.'

'Honey,' said Piglet to himself in a thoughtful way, as if it were now settled. '*I'll* dig the pit, while *you* go and get the honey.'

'Very well,' said Pooh, and he stumped off.

As soon as he got home, he went to

the larder; and he stood on a chair, and took down a very large jar of honey from the top shelf. It had HUNNY written on it, but, just to make sure, he took off the paper cover and looked at it, and it *looked* just like honey. 'But you never can tell,' said Pooh. 'I remember my uncle saying once that he had seen cheese just this colour.' So he put his tongue in, and took a large lick. 'Yes,' he said, 'it is. No doubt about that. And honey, I should say, right down to the bottom of the jar. Unless, of course,' he said, 'somebody put cheese in at the bottom just for a joke. Perhaps I had better go a *little* further ... just in case ... in case Heffalumps *don't* like cheese ... same as me ... Ah!' And he gave a deep sigh. 'I *was* right. It *is* honey, right the way down.'

Having made certain of this, he took the jar back to Piglet, and Piglet looked up from the bottom of his Very Deep Pit, and said, 'Got it?' and Pooh said, 'Yes,

but it isn't quite a full jar,'
and he threw it down to
Piglet, and Piglet said, 'No,
it isn't! Is that all you've got
left?' and Pooh said, 'Yes.' Because
it was. So Piglet put the jar at the bottom
of the Pit, and climbed out, and they
went off home together.

'Well, good night, Pooh,' said
Piglet, when they had got to
Pooh's house. 'And we meet
at six o'clock tomorrow

morning by the Pine Trees, and see how many Heffalumps we've got in our Trap.'

'Six o'clock, Piglet. And have you got any string?'

'No. Why do you want string?'

'To lead them home with.'

'Oh! ... I *think* Heffalumps come if you whistle.'

'Some do and some don't. You never can tell with Heffalumps. Well, good night!'

'Good night!'

And off Piglet trotted to his house TRESPASSERS W, while Pooh made his preparations for bed.

Some hours later, just as the night was beginning to steal away, Pooh woke up suddenly with a sinking feeling. He had had that sinking feeling before, and he knew what it meant. *He was hungry.* So he went to the larder, and he stood on a chair and reached up to the top shelf, and found – nothing.

'That's funny,' he thought. 'I know

I had a jar of honey there. A full jar, full of honey right up to the top, and it had HUNNY written on it, so that I should know it was honey. That's very funny.' And then he began to wander up and down, wondering where it was and murmuring a murmur to himself. Like this:

*It's very, very funny*
*'Cos I know I had some honey;*
*'Cos it had a label on,*

*Saying HUNNY.*
*A goloptious full-up pot too,*
*And I don't know where it's got to,*
*No, I don't know where it's gone –*
*Well, it's funny.*

He had murmured this to himself three times in a singing sort of way, when suddenly he remembered. He had put it into the Cunning Trap to catch the Heffalump.

'Bother!' said Pooh. 'It all comes

of trying to be kind to Heffalumps.' And he got back into bed.

But he couldn't sleep. The more he tried to sleep, the more he couldn't. He tried Counting Sheep, which is sometimes a good way of getting to sleep, and, as that was no good, he tried counting Heffalumps. And that was worse. Because every Heffalump that he counted was making straight for a pot of Pooh's honey, *and eating it all*. For some minutes he lay there miserably, but when the five hundred and eighty-seventh Heffalump was licking its jaws, and saying to itself, 'Very good honey this, I don't know when I've tasted better,' Pooh could bear it no longer. He jumped out of bed, he ran out of the house, and he ran straight to the Six Pine Trees.

The Sun was still in bed, but there was a lightness in the sky over the Hundred Acre Wood which seemed to show that it was waking up and would soon be kicking off the clothes. In the half-light

the Pine Trees looked cold and lonely, and the Very Deep Pit seemed deeper than it was, and Pooh's jar of honey at the bottom was something mysterious, a shape and no more. But as he got nearer to it his nose told him that it was indeed honey, and his tongue came out and began to polish up his mouth, ready for it.

'Bother!' said Pooh, as he got his nose inside the jar. 'A Heffalump has been eating it!' And then he thought a little and said, 'Oh, no, *I* did. I forgot.'

Indeed, he had eaten most of it. But there was a little left at the very bottom of the jar, and he pushed his head right in, and began to lick ...

By and by Piglet woke up. As soon as he woke he said to himself, 'Oh!' Then he said bravely, 'Yes,' and then, still more bravely, 'Quite so.' But he didn't feel very brave, for the word which was really jiggeting about in his brain was 'Heffalumps'.

What was a Heffalump like?

Was it Fierce?

*Did* it come when you whistled? And *how* did it come?

Was it Fond of Pigs at all?

If it was Fond of Pigs, did it make any difference *what sort of Pig?*

Supposing it was Fierce with Pigs, would it make any difference *if the Pig had a grandfather called TRESPASSERS WILLIAM?*

He didn't know the answer to any of these questions ... and he was going to see his first Heffalump in about an hour from now!

Of course Pooh would be with him, and it was much more Friendly with two. But suppose Heffalumps were Very Fierce with Pigs *and* Bears? Wouldn't it be better to pretend that he had a headache, and couldn't go up to the Six Pine Trees this morning? But then suppose that it was a very fine day, and there was no Heffalump in the trap, here he would be, in bed all the morning, simply wasting his time for nothing. What should he do?

And then he had a Clever Idea. He would go up very quietly to the Six Pine Trees now, peep very cautiously into the

Trap, and see if there *was* a Heffalump there. And if there was, he would go back to bed, and if there wasn't, he wouldn't.

So off he went. At first he thought that there wouldn't be a Heffalump in the Trap, and then he thought that there would, and as he got nearer he was *sure* that there would, because he could hear it heffalumping about like anything.

'Oh, dear, oh, dear, oh, dear!' said Piglet to himself. And he wanted to run away. But somehow, having got so near, he felt that he must just see what a Heffalump was like. So he crept to the side of the Trap and looked in ...

And all the time Winnie-the-Pooh had been trying to get the honey-jar off his head. The more he shook it, the more tightly it stuck. '*Bother!*' he said, inside the jar, and '*Oh, help!*' and, mostly, '*Ow!*' And he tried bumping it against things, but as he couldn't see what he was bumping it against, it didn't help him; and he tried to climb out of the

Trap, but as he could see nothing but jar, and not much of that, he couldn't find his way. So at last he lifted up his head, jar and all, and made a loud, roaring noise of Sadness and Despair ... and it was at that moment that Piglet looked down.

'Help, help!' cried Piglet, 'a Heffalump, a Horrible Heffalump!' and he scampered off as hard as he could, still crying out, 'Help, help, a Herrible Hoffalump! Hoff, Hoff, a Hellible Horralump! Holl, Holl, a Hoffable Hellerump!' And he didn't stop crying and scampering until he got to Christopher Robin's house.

'Whatever's the matter, Piglet?' said Christopher Robin, who was just getting up.

'Heff,' said Piglet, breathing so hard

that he could hardly speak, 'A Heff – a Heff – a Heffalump.'

'Where?'

'Up there,' said Piglet, waving his paw. 'What did it look like?'

'Like – like – It had the biggest head you ever saw, Christopher Robin. A great enormous thing, like – like nothing. A huge big – well, like a – I don't know – like an enormous big nothing. Like a jar.'

'Well,' said Christopher Robin, putting on his shoes, 'I shall go and look at it. Come on.'

Piglet wasn't afraid if he had Christopher Robin with him, so off they went ...

'I can hear it, can't you?' said Piglet anxiously, as they got near.

'I can hear *something*,' said Christopher Robin.

It was Pooh bumping his head against a tree-root he had found.

'There!' said Piglet. 'Isn't it *awful?*' And he held on tight to Christopher

Robin's hand.

Suddenly Christopher Robin began to laugh ... and he laughed ... and he laughed ... and he laughed. And while he was still laughing – *Crash* went the Heffalump's head against the tree-root, *Smash* went the jar, and out came Pooh's head again ...

Then Piglet saw what a Foolish Piglet he had been, and he was so ashamed of himself that he ran straight off home

and went to bed with a headache.

But Christopher Robin and Pooh went home to breakfast together.

'Oh, Bear!' said Christopher Robin. 'How I do love you!'

'So do I,' said Pooh.

*The End*